MW00897125

*For my mentors Joanne and Frieda*
*And for my contrarian sisters Mary Anne and Mariella*
*—T.H.*

*For my mom*
*—R.B.*

by Theo Heras

Illustrations by Renné Benoit

pajamapress

Time for bed.
Pick up toys and
put them away.

Where's Bunny?

Bath next.

Warm water
tickles toes.

Rubber ducky dunks and swims.

Little sheep squirts.

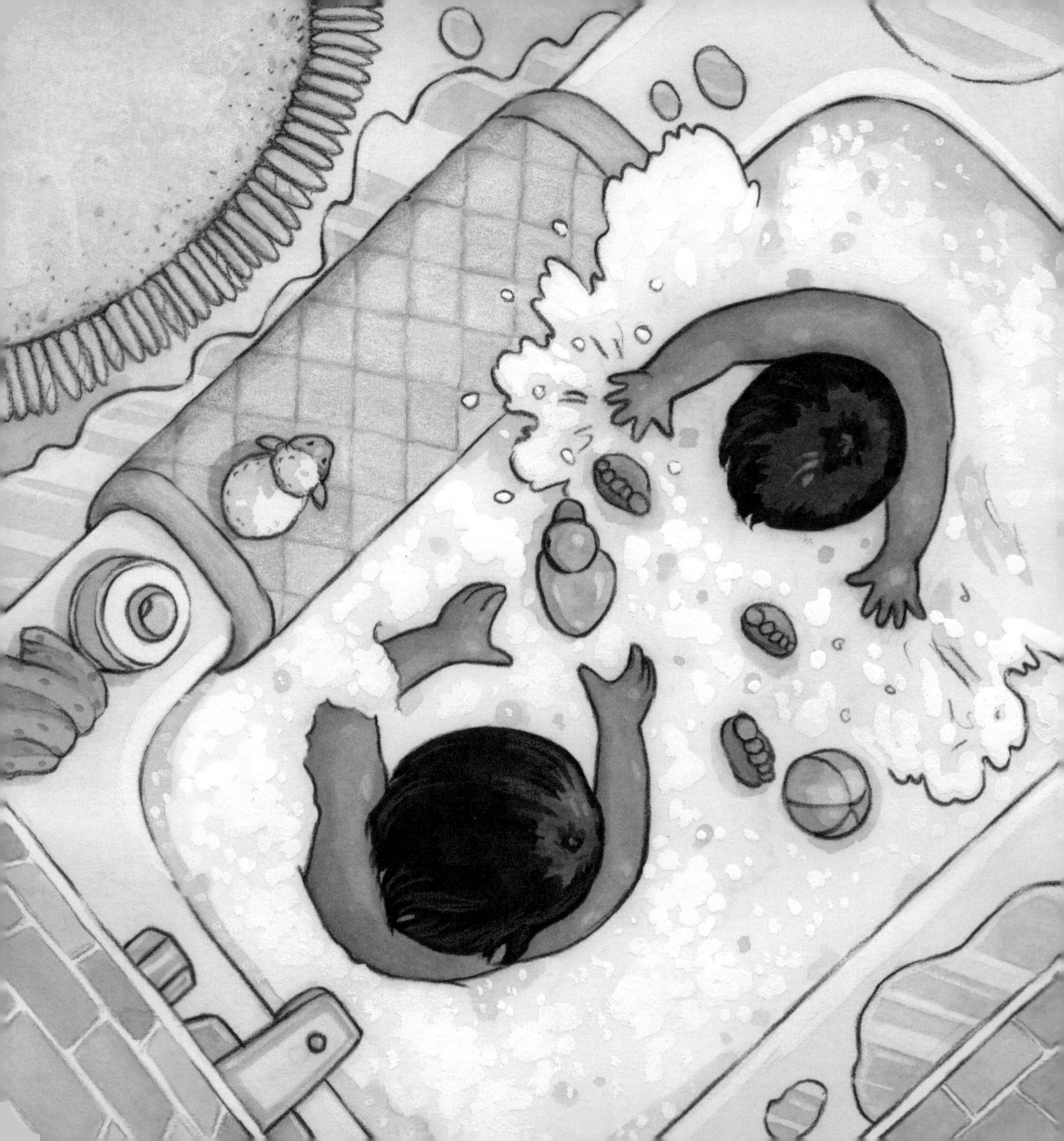

Wet all over.

Swimming!

Uh-oh. Wash hair.

Soapy suds,
not in eyes!

All done.
Out of the
tub.

# Wrap up warm and dry. Where's Bunny?

# Clean teeth.

Jump into cozy
jammies.

Where's Bunny?

Snuggle in bed
to hear a favorite
story and sing
a favorite song.

Again! Again!

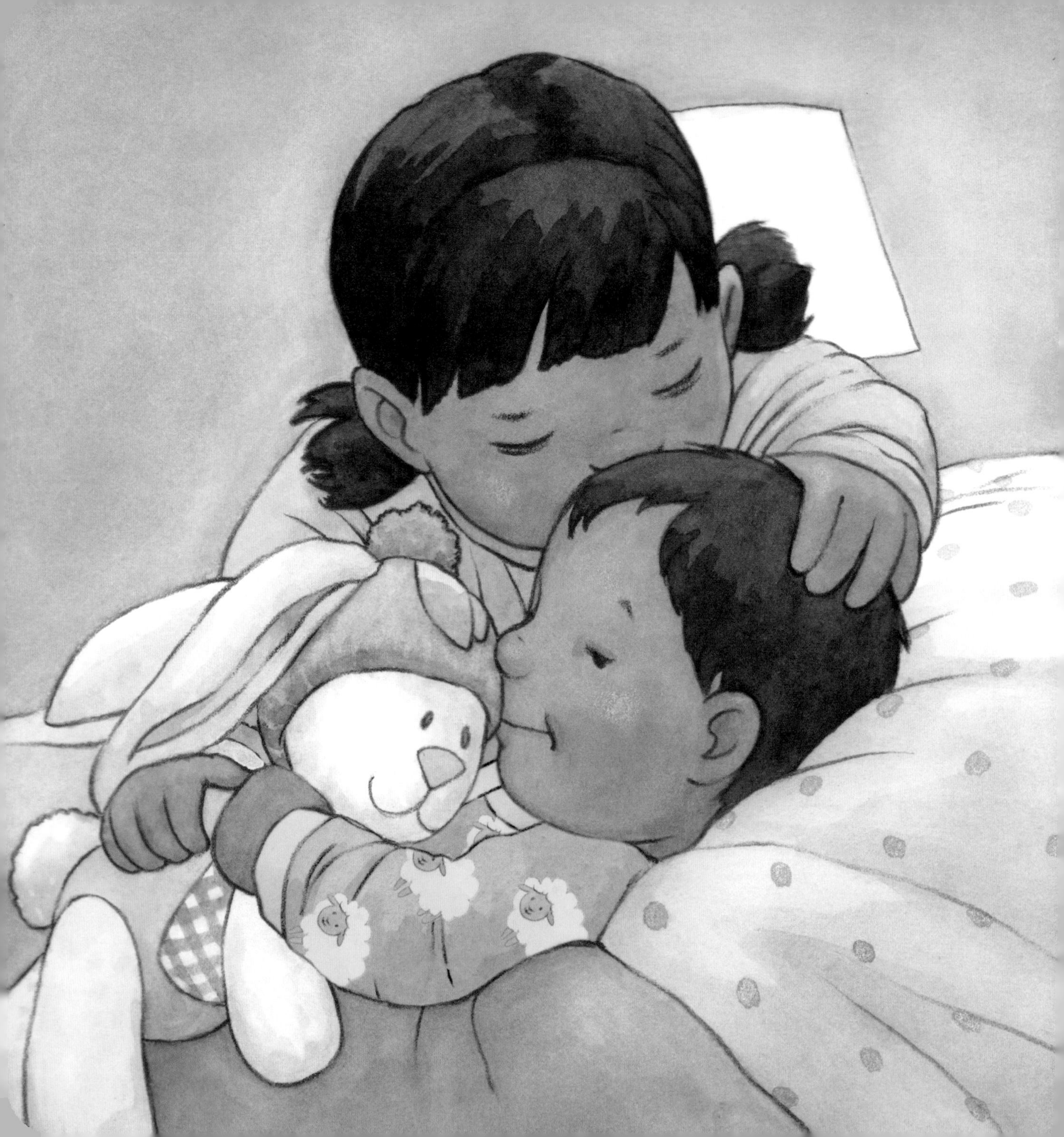

Hugs and kisses.

All is well.

# Good night, Bunny.

**First published in Canada and the United States in 2018**



This is a first edition.

10 9 8 7 6 5 4 3 2 1



www.pajamapress.ca info@pajamapress.ca

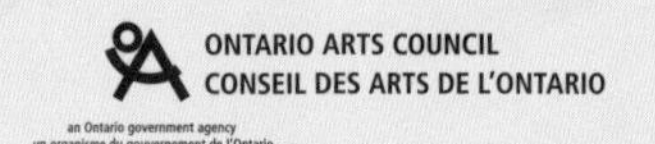


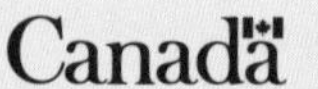


The publisher gratefully acknowledges the support of the Canada Council for the Arts and the Ontario Arts Council for its publishing program. We acknowledge the financial support of the Government of Canada through the Canada Book Fund (CBF) for our publishing activities.

**Library and Archives Canada Cataloguing in Publication**

Heras, Theo, author
Where's Bunny? / by Theo Heras ; illustrations by Renné Benoit.
ISBN 978-1-77278-043-7 (hardcover)
I. Benoit, Renné, illustrator II. Title. III. Title: Where is Bunny?
PS8615.E687W44 2018 jC813'.6 C2017-905671-9

**Publisher Cataloging-in-Publication Data (U.S.)**

Names: Heras, Theo, 1948-, author. | Benoit, Renné, illustrator.
Title: Where's Bunny? / by Theo Heras ; illustrations by Renné Benoit.
Description: Toronto, Ontario Canada : Pajama Press, 2018. | Summary: "Helped by his big sister, Baby and his stuffed bunny navigate the bedtime routine including bath, story, song, and goodnight kisses and hugs"— Provided by publisher.
Identifiers: ISBN 978-1-77278-043-7 (hardcover)
Subjects: LCSH: Brothers and sisters – Juvenile fiction. | Bedtime – Juvenile fiction. | Humorous stories. | BISAC: JUVENILE FICTION / Bedtime & Dreams. | JUVENILE FICTION / Family / Siblings.
Classification: LCC PZ7.H473Whe |DDC [E] – dc23

Designed by Rebecca Bender

Manufactured by Qualibre Inc./Printplus
Printed in China

**Pajama Press Inc.**
181 Carlaw Ave. Suite 207 Toronto, Ontario Canada, M4M 2S1

Distributed in Canada by UTP Distribution
5201 Dufferin Street Toronto, Ontario Canada, M3H 5T8

Distributed in the U.S. by Ingram Publisher Services
1 Ingram Blvd. La Vergne, TN 37086, USA

**Original art created in watercolor and digital**